The
TRIALS
OF
RUBY P. BAXTER

Joanna Nadin

Illustrated by Gemma Correll

OXFORD
UNIVERSITY PRESS

KEEP OUT
(That means you, Topaz!)

Important EVIDENCE to prove that the life of me, Ruby P. Baxter, aged 10^1/$_4$, is exceedingly TRYING.

(If lost, please return to:
Ruby P. Baxter,
67, Arkwright Avenue,
Chipping Broadley

i.e. the house with the bit of car in the front garden and the shed that looks kind of exploded, which Dad says he is going to fix, but he also said that about my bicycle and Topaz's hair straighteners and the microwave. Only the bicycle still has just one wheel, the hair straighteners actually cook your hair, and the microwave doesn't cook anything at all, ever since Dad put his patented boiled egg maker in there, which now also needs fixing.)

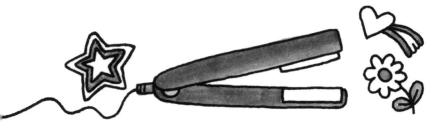

4

Sunday 10th June
(Last day of the holidays)

Things that are exceedingly trying today:

1. Dad got all excited because he claimed he had finally fixed my bicycle, but it turns out he has fixed it with a wheel from my old pram, which is too small, so now it slopes backwards really weirdly. He said it doesn't matter what it looks like, as long as it is safe to ride. Only I tried to ride it and fell off three times. Mum says this does not bode well for Dad's plans to become an entrepreneur, so now they are not speaking to each other and I have three bruises on my leg.

OLD PRAM
WHEEL
(THANKS DAD!)

2.   I was supposed to go to Elsie Eckersley's (i.e. my best friend) for tea today, only she is stuck on a plane on a runway in somewhere called Alicante so I am stuck with cheese on toast and half a biscuit. It is a wonder I don't get rickets or scurvy. Mrs Hunderby, our headmistress, says it is almost impossible to get diseases like that now as it is the 21st century, but she hasn't been to our house.

NORMAL PETS

chomp

3.   I will never even get to be stuck on a
runway, let alone go on a real holiday abroad, e.g.
to Florida in six weeks to visit Gran and her new
husband, Hank, because the goat has eaten my
passport. Other people have normal pets like cats
or dogs or hamsters, whereas I have a goat called
Arnold Laine. I mean, what sort of name is that
for an animal? Plus so far this month he has
eaten two wellington boots, the remote control
from the TV and Topaz's pearl earrings. Mum
said she could just wait for them to come out the
other end, but Topaz said she would rather die.

4.   My middle name is so ridiculous I cannot even write it down.

At least Topaz isn't here. She is at the park with Shanice Reynolds watching Garth Hunt play football. They are both in love with him. I do not know why. He has a face like a ferret and he picks his nose. I have seen him.

But, even without Topaz, I am almost glad to be going back to school tomorrow because it cannot possibly be any worse than 67, Arkwright Avenue.

Monday 11th June
(First day of school)
I was wrong. Because even though school doesn't have a goat, or a sloping bicycle, or Topaz, it does have my absolute mortal enemy, i.e. Lacey Prendergast. Lacey has two cats, pierced ears

and her dad has a real job, i.e. he owns a chain of pet shops called Prendergast's Pets. Plus she is in all the posters for Prendergast's, which she says makes her famous, but Elsie says makes her a show-off.

Today she was showing off about her new pet, which is a pony called Titus. She says he has won ten red rosettes and can jump over a fence as tall as Harriet Juniper (who is one metre forty). I was thinking that Arnold Laine could probably eat a fence as tall as Harriet Juniper, as well as Harriet herself, but I didn't say it out loud because if she found out I had a goat for a pet I would be a laughing stock for weeks.

Our teacher, Mr Atkins, said he had something to announce, which was that Lulu Webster-Price, who is Lacey's best friend and who has pierced ears, a parrot and a swimming pool, has left to go to Pennington Academy for Girls. I almost felt sorry for Lacey, because I know if Elsie was leaving I would be mortified. But Lacey said she was going to beg her dad to send her there, because they have horse riding instead of netball, and everyone has a laptop instead of sharing the computer with the Y key missing, so I am back to thinking she is trying. And Mr Atkins thinks so too.

Also Elsie says Mrs Hunderby is wrong about scurvy because, according to her mum, who is a nurse, someone called Mrs Tippit from Rigby Road had it last year. I said her mum wasn't supposed to tell her stuff like that, because of confidentiality, but she says she didn't tell her – she overheard her mum on the phone to her Aunty Jean.

Tuesday 12th June

I think I might have rickets after all as my legs were especially wobbly in netball today and I fell over twice. Lacey, who is team captain, said I might as well be replaced with Topov, who is the school rabbit and who only has three legs. I said it would be better if we replaced Lacey with Grimble, who was also a school rabbit, only now it is actually dead. This made me and Elsie laugh so much I didn't see Delia Frink throw the ball to me, which hit me on the head and I fell over again.

Wednesday 13th June
8am

Dad is going to see his friend Dave the Rave today, which means Mum is in a bad mood, which means I have got peanut butter and tuna sandwiches for lunch because she couldn't concentrate. This is because every time Dad goes to see Dave the Rave he comes back with something he claims is the key to our fortune, but

Mum claims is a blooming nuisance, e.g.

1. Fourteen exercise bicycles, which he claimed he was going to use to turn our garage into a gym, only the men from the council said he needed a licence, and lights, as it was so dark in there one of them walked into a door.

2. A giant saucepan and seventy-two punnets of strawberries, which he claimed he was going to turn into jam and then sell to the expensive deli on the corner of Armitage Street. Only it turns out he doesn't know how to make jam and we ended up eating strawberry soup for tea for months. If I even look at a strawberry now, I feel sick. Topaz says if she even looks at one, she will die.

3. Arnold Laine, who Dad claimed was going to keep us in milk. Only Arnold turned out to be a boy, and they don't do milk, they just eat weird stuff and headbutt walls. (This isn't just a goat thing – I have seen Brady O'Grady drink ketchup and bang his head against the canteen wall to prove how manly he is.)

Dad has promised not to bring back anything useless, but both me and Mum fear the worst.

5pm

Mum and I were right. Dad has come home with an old motor, which he says he is going to turn into a generator and we will never have to pay another electricity bill again. Only it turns out he is intending to fuel the generator with animal manure, except Arnold does not make enough, so now he is begging Mum to get a cow. She says over her dead body. Arnold Laine is enough trouble as it is (today he got his foot stuck in a flowerpot, so he was banging it on the floor and bleating madly, which made Mrs Duckworth next door threaten to call the police), so it is back to the drawing board for Dad.

Mum has brought something home from work too. It is nits, which she says she must have got off Alfie Garfunkel, who is always scratching. Mum works at the local nursery, which means she is mostly getting nits and pulling pieces of macaroni out of noses. (Alfie Garfunkel is always doing this as well.) I am never having children – they are far too trying. Plus why can't my parents have normal jobs like Elsie's mum and dad, who are both nurses? She says actually it's not that great, because they talk about diseases all the time, and once about a man who had a worm that was fifty centimetres long living in his stomach, which was gross. But at least worms don't get stuck in flowerpots.

On the plus side, Elsie swapped my tuna and peanut butter sandwich for her cheese and cucumber one. She is weird, which is why we are so good at being best friends.

UGH!

Thursday 14th June

School was especially trying today because of country dancing, i.e. dancing to folk songs with boys. I do not know why Mr Atkins makes us do this because no one likes it – the boys think dancing is for girls, and the girls think they are going to catch the Dreaded Lurgy from having to hold the boys' hands. Mr Atkins said the Dreaded Lurgy isn't real, but Elsie said lurgies are actually very real and can be anything from common flu to a flesh-eating supervirus. Lacey said the sooner she went to Pennington the better, because they don't have boys at all, which means no superviruses, and even I had to agree with that. Boys are the most trying thing of all, e.g.

1. Dad, who is trying to fuel his generator with the contents of the kitchen bin, only all that has happened so far is that the shed smells of burnt cheese.

2.   Arnold Laine, who spent the day with a flowerpot on his head, only when I went to take it off, he ran away. I think he thinks he has an excellent hat.

3.   Brady O'Grady, who I had to do the do-si-do with, only he do-sied too hard and I went flying into a crash mat and everyone cheered.

Admittedly Topaz, who was very trying today, is not a boy, but her trouble is because of a boy, i.e. Garth Hunt, who did not even look at her in the spaghetti queue at lunchtime. She has begged Mum to let her dye her hair so she is more noticeable. Mum says she is not dying anything, not after the last fiasco, and she should be happy to stand out for who she is, not what she looks like. So Topaz said that no one understands her and shut herself in her room again. She is right. I do not understand her at all.

Friday 15th June

School was even more trying today and it is because of a boy.

It all started when Mr Atkins said we had a new project for the rest of the term and it is World War 2. Immediately all the boys started shooting each other with rulers and pretending to die horribly with blood spurting from their mortal wounds. Only Mr Atkins said we would mostly be learning about what it was like on the home front, i.e. growing extra vegetables and making parachutes rather than actual fighting, and so they stopped dying and said, 'Ohhhhhhh' in whiny voices. Then it was my turn to say 'Ohhhhhh' because Mr Atkins said we couldn't pick our own partners this time – he was going to mix us up because the war was all about tolerance.

Brady O'Grady said actually the war was all about shooting people and then the boys started dying horribly again, so Mr Atkins shut him up by making him work with Georgina Lupin. But just as I was thinking *phew* because it meant I didn't have to work with Brady O'Grady, Mr Atkins read my name out and said I would be working with Edward Bean.

Bean

Admittedly, he does not bang his head against walls or drink ketchup (not that I have seen), but he is still a boy.

Elsie said in fact it is her I should be feeling sorry for, as she has to work with Lacey Prendergast. But I said last time I did a project with Lacey, i.e. on animals of Africa, her dad hired an actual snake and a mongoose, which she brought into school, and so she is bound to get five gold stars, while I am in hospital with the Dreaded Lurgy.

Saturday 16th June

Today is definitely less trying because:

1. Topaz has gone to Dress to Impress with Shanice to try on very small skirts for the end of term disco, even though it is not for five weeks. She is hoping there is a purple one, because purple is Garth's favourite colour according to Shanice, who got it off Verity Jones, who got it off her brother Charley, who plays football with Garth.

VERY SHORT

2. Dad has gone to Dave the Rave's, so, even though he is bound to bring something bonkers back, at least he is not doing anything bonkers right now.

3. Arnold Laine is busy licking the fence, which is slightly bonkers, but not as bonkers as eating it.

4. Mum has got rid of her nits. I am not sure where, but she says they are definitely gone.

5pm

I have found out where the nits went. It is onto my head and now I am itching, and Topaz is back from town and is killing herself laughing. Dad has brought a special bottle of pet shampoo  back from Dave the Rave's for Arnold Laine and he is saying he can use it to banish the nits. All of which completely proves that I have worse luck than anyone else in the world ever.

Sunday 17th June

Arnold Laine has escaped again. Mrs Duckworth is livid because he has eaten her husband Bert's vest and pants off her washing line. Mum has had to pay her £5 to make up for it, which Dad says is ridiculous because, by the look of the rest of Bert's clothes, Mrs Duckworth bought them in World War 2, when they only cost tuppence. But Mum said Dad is in no position to say anything as he is the one who brought Arnold home in the first place and, if he doesn't sort him out, Arnold will have to go and live on a farm, i.e. where goats are supposed to live. Dad says that would be a disaster as Arnold is the key to our fortune. I do not know how, unless it is in a circus as ARNOLD – the All-Eating Phenomegoat.

ARNOLD

THE ALL-EATING PHENOMEGOAT!

Monday 18th June

I told Elsie about the nits, which have gone (with nit shampoo, NOT goat shampoo), but even so, I am sure I can still feel them. She says it would be worse luck if I had, e.g. the giant worm in my stomach, or parasites in my brain, or a spider living under my skin, which her mum actually saw once and it was gross. And I suppose it is true, but I bet none of those people also had Topaz or a goat to annoy them.

Tuesday 19th June

Edward Bean agrees with Elsie about nits not being so bad. He said every year 2,900 people are killed by hippos and 11 people are killed by vending machines so, if you think about it, I am lucky really. I said it was only luck that a hippo hadn't wandered into Chipping Broadley because, if it did, I bet it would be me that got trodden on and squished. Edward thought this was funny, but I don't know why because being trodden on by an escaped hippo is deadly serious.

We were working on our World War 2 project, i.e. imagining what it is like in an air raid. Mr Atkins used the playground bell as an air raid warning and every time it rang we had to hide under the tables, which were our shelters, in less than ten seconds. Only I tripped over Stephen Millican's foot and got tangled in some chair

legs so it took me fifteen seconds, which meant I would definitely have been bombed. Brady O'Grady said in fact we should have real bombs, e.g. custard pies, or water balloons, but Mr Atkins said under no circumstances is he to assemble any weapons because if he tried it, Mr Atkins would go straight to Mrs Hunderby, so at least I have that to be grateful for.

Wednesday 20th June

Even with the bombs, I think it would be less trying to live in World War 2 than it is to live at 67, Arkwright Avenue today. This is because no one is speaking to anyone, e.g.

1. Topaz is not speaking to Mum because Mum said she cannot go to Charley Jones' party on Saturday night, even though Garth Hunt will be there, because Nanna Baxter is coming to dinner.

2. Mum is not speaking to Dad because he invited Nanna Baxter to dinner without asking her, and Nanna Baxter is especially trying because she does not eat anything suspicious or out of a packet, which is most things in this house. Plus she has a moustache.

3.   Dad is not speaking to anyone because he is busy with something in the shed. Mum said he better not be trying to invent a Patented Breakfast-Making Machine again, because last time he did that he short-circuited the electricity. We had no lights or hot water for a week. Topaz couldn't use her hairdryer and she said she'd rather die than have untameable hair again.

I hope that is what Dad is doing. Even though I don't want Topaz to die, having no electricity would be very war-like and I would get extra points on my project.

Thursday 21st June
I have changed my mind about wanting to live in the war. According to Mr Atkins, it was completely normal for people to have farm animals in their back gardens, so they could have extra milk and meat because of rationing, which is where people were only allowed, e.g. eight ounces of meat a week. I said that was better than in our house because I haven't seen any meat in our fridge for a month, which made Edward Bean laugh again. He is weird if you ask me.

I could tell that Elsie really wanted to tell Mr Atkins about Arnold Laine because she kept nudging me when he was talking about his grandma having a chicken in her garden. But I said if she ever told anyone then it would be the end of the world and also our friendship. But, luckily, I know this is never going to happen.

Friday 22nd June

Last year, we had Mrs Tipton as a class teacher and even though she said me and Elsie were always in cahoots, i.e. up to no good (which was not even true, except once, when we were thinking up ways to give Lacey Prendergast brain parasites), I wish we still had her because she would never ever have done what Mr Atkins did today.

We were just packing away the paint things after doing a giant mural of London in an air raid (which had to be re-done because Mr Atkins told Brady O'Grady that Buckingham Palace did not get trampled on by giant dinosaurs, which weren't even alive in World War 2; only Brady said it would have been good if they were alive, and also on our side, because then we would have won, which Mr Atkins said we did anyway without the dinosaurs, which Brady said was disappointing) when Mr Atkins said, 'Oh, I just remembered, at the end of term we are going to have a Gang Show.'

And then everyone went very quiet because none of us knew what a Gang Show was. So Mr Atkins told us it was what people did for entertainment in the war, i.e. before they had televisions and games consoles, and even all the soldiers did it too. What happens is that all of us will have a turn to go up on stage and sing or dance or do an act that shows off our special talents. Only the thing is I do not have any special talents, unless you count putting up with Topaz, which I am pretty sure Mr Atkins does not.

Saturday 23rd June
Mum says I am being pessimistic, i.e. looking on the dark side, because everyone has at least one special talent, even Dad (although sometimes it

is quite hard to tell, especially when he has been spending all day doing something with a running machine that Dave the Rave got from the tip). I asked what Dad's special talent was and Mum said he can sing all the names of the planets in our solar system in a song, which he did. Only he was on the running machine at the time and he lost concentration and fell off backwards so 'Jupiter' was more of a scream.

Mum can dance the tango, which she did, with Dad, only he was still hobbling from the Jupiter incident. Topaz can do the splits, only she didn't, because she was still sulking over not going to Charley Jones' party because of Nanna Baxter. And it turns out even Nanna Baxter has a special talent (and it is not having a moustache), i.e. she can tap dance to 'New York, New York'. Only she didn't because she was cross about the fish fingers because they are from a packet.

But when I tried to do their talents they all went wrong, i.e.

1.   When I tried to do Dad's planet song, I could only remember Mars and Pluto so it was very short.

2.   When I tried to do Mum's tango, I accidentally whirled into the mantelpiece and knocked over a picture of Topaz dressed as a snowflake.

3. When I tried to do Topaz's splits, I got stuck halfway down and Dad had to rescue me before I snapped in half.

4. When I tried to do Nanna's tap dance, I couldn't because Arnold Laine had eaten a bit of the CD player and no one knew the tune properly.

Mum said I was looking at it all wrong, i.e. I had to find my own talent, not borrow someone else's, and I am bound to find one as I have hidden depths. But what if mine is hidden so deep I don't find it in time for the Gang Show? Mum said she is sure that whatever I do I will stand out anyway, and that is what matters. But I don't want to stand out. I'd rather just fit in. Or even disappear altogether.

Sunday 24th June

Today it is Topaz's turn to want to disappear. She is especially trying because Suzy Gilhoolie called to tell her what happened at Charley Jones' party last night. Suzy said that she heard it off Stacey Nugent, who heard it off Verity Jones, who heard it off Charley, that Garth Hunt kissed Shanice, which Topaz says is the ultimate betrayal. So now she has no best friend and no boyfriend and she'd rather die than ever go to school again. I said what about Suzy Gilhoolie then? But Topaz says she makes a funny noise when she eats, plus her favourite band is The Beast when everyone knows Pink Lemonade is the best.

I said I was sorry she was sad and I know I'd feel terrible if Elsie ever kissed a boy I liked, only that will never happen because: a) I don't like a boy and b) Elsie is my best friend. Only Topaz said I was fooling myself and it will happen one day, whether I like it or not. It is called being a grown-up.

I hope I never grow up.

Monday 25th June

Topaz has gone to school after all. Mum said she could only stay off if she had an actual illness – being lovesick does not count and nor does sticking the thermometer in hot water to pretend you have a temperature.

I wish I had an actual illness because everyone in our class has gone Gang Show MAD and they are all talking about what they are going to do as their special talent, e.g.

1. Luke Bruton said he is going to impersonate Mrs Hunderby.

2. Kyle McKiver said he is going to break-dance.

3. Lacey Prendergast said she and Georgia-May Mannering are going to sing 'It's a Long Way to Tipperary' and they are going to win first prize, i.e. a glittering trophy.

Only Mr Atkins said that it was a GANG Show, not a TV talent show, so there was no glittering trophy or any prize at all, except the joy of knowing you had cheered everyone up. Then everyone said, 'Ohhhhhhhh' in their whiny voices and Brady O'Grady said it was worse than being in the actual war. Lacey said she wasn't going to do it at all because she has to say 'Prendergast's: it's the best for pets!' in a radio advert in three weeks and she doesn't want to damage her voice just on account of some joy.

So, in the end, Mr Atkins said he would do rosettes for first, second and third and everyone would get a piece of barley sugar, which is a sweet they had in the war (but hardly any because of rationing, which Brady O'Grady said was worse than being bombed).

Lacey Prendergast is bound to win. She already has ten rosettes, whereas the only thing I won was a toy yacht in the church raffle last year and that sank.

Tuesday 26th June

Even Edward Bean has a talent. He can multiply any two numbers in his head in just seconds, e.g. 37×71, which is 2,627. Lacey Prendergast said that is not a proper talent – it has to be singing or dancing, but Edward said anything is a talent if you do it really well even just being able to balance a ruler on your nose (which we tried and neither of us can).

I asked Elsie what she was doing for her talent, but she says she is not sure yet. She will probably do 'Name that Symptom', i.e. when we all shout out things like 'sore throat' or 'rash on your fingers' and she tells you three diseases that you might have. Brady O'Grady is not allowed to do any shouting out because last time he kept shouting 'bad at football', which Elsie said wasn't a symptom of anything, but Brady said Luke Bruton has it and he will soon have another symptom, i.e. 'head fallen off' if he doesn't score against Nailton on Saturday, so he got sent to Mrs Hunderby.

Wednesday 27th June

I still haven't found my talent. I tried playing Topaz's violin when I got home from school, but the A string snapped and Topaz went mad and said I owed her at least £10 and it is yet more evidence that the world is against her. I said the world is against me actually, but Mum said it is against all the Baxters. Dad has a sore hand from when he got it trapped in the fence as he was trying to help Arnold Laine, whose head was trapped in the fence. Mum has got wet socks because Alfie Garfunkel blocked the sink at nursery with paper towels to try to create the sea and now the toilets are flooded. I said maybe that was his special talent, which made Dad laugh until he choked on a pea, but Mum didn't see the funny side.

Esca-pea!

Thursday 28th June
8am

I am going to ask Elsie if we can work together on the talent show, e.g. she can teach me lots of diseases and we can both do 'Name that Symptom'. Or I can do some really difficult things for her to guess, like 'fear of water' (which is rabies, which you get from wild animals, only not Arnold Laine, I have checked). Mum said that wasn't really showing the world how special I am, but I said the only special thing about me is the weirdness, which I'd rather not show anyone, and anyway, being a double act is more fun.

5pm

I'm not going to do the double act after all. Elsie says she is going to sing 'It's a Long Way to Tipperary' with Lacey and Georgia-May as they are going to be a girl band. I said that was weird because she didn't even like Lacey, but she says she's not that bad once you get to know her,

e.g. she is letting Elsie ride her pony, Titus, on Sunday.

I said I thought she was coming to my house for tea on Sunday and we were going to make Everything Biscuits, i.e. where you get everything from the food cupboard and add different combinations to the biscuit mix to test out what works and what doesn't (e.g. coconut and raspberry works, and marmalade and mustard doesn't). She said maybe another time and then Lacey showed up and said she had to hurry up because they needed to practise doo-wops. I said maybe I could come and all four of us could sing together, but Lacey said no because no one ever heard of a girl band with four people in it, plus she only has three silver headbands anyway.

When I got home, Topaz said, 'I told you so, it is the ultimate betrayal.' I said it wasn't, it was just because no one ever heard of a girl band with four people in it, but Topaz said what about Pink Lemonade and I didn't have an answer to that. Luckily I didn't need one because at that exact moment we heard Mrs Duckworth wail madly and we all ran out to find Arnold Laine headbutting her back door. Mrs Duckworth said he was trying to do her in. Dad said it was probably just the trifle on the kitchen table as he is partial to custard, only Mrs Duckworth didn't look happy about that either. Dad has shut Arnold in his pen with his Patented Padlock, which he says is unbeatable.

Friday 29th June

Mr Atkins has given us homework for the weekend. He says he wants us to work in our pairs and make Woolton Pie, which is what everyone had in the war for a feast. Edward said he could come to my house if I liked. But I didn't like, because it means he would find out about my dad and his mad inventions AND Arnold Laine AND my mum not being able to cook anything, not even Woolton Pie. So I am going to his house at 12, Prentice Place instead.

When I got home, I knew I had made the right decision because Arnold Laine had eaten the Patented Padlock and was out of his pen and back in disgrace again.

Saturday 30th June

Edward's house isn't at all trying, i.e. the taps don't fall off when you turn them, so water doesn't spurt on the ceiling, and he doesn't have a sister who says she would rather die than lend you her pink gel pen, or a goat who then eats the pink gel pen anyway. He has a mum and dad who wear normal clothes, i.e. T-shirts and jeans instead of binbags and rain hats (the tap at home just will not shut off). He has a dog called Raffles who eats dog food and dog food only, and he doesn't have a brother or sister,  i.e. he is an only child. He is so lucky. Edward says it isn't lucky at all – it's actually a bit boring. But how can it be boring to have chairs that do not suddenly tip you out because a leg has fallen off?

It turns out Woolton Pie tastes a bit like soggy bathroom sponge. Though I said bathroom sponges would probably be nicer because at least they aren't gritty, plus they don't rot your teeth, which made Edward Bean laugh, even though I wasn't actually joking. Then we practised Edward's talent and he even got 29 × 92, which is almost as good as knowing the symptoms of Spanish Flu. But only almost.

He said maybe I should try juggling, because he had seen a man on TV last night juggling five fire sticks and it was amazing and he got maximum points. I said it was a good idea and I would try it when I got home. Only not with fire, as Mum is still cross after the time Dad set the kitchen alight. I will use soft balls or scarves.

AMAZING!

NOT
ON FIRE!

MUM'S
SCARVES

Sunday 1st July

The juggling did not go according to plan,
i.e. several very trying things happened:

1. We didn't have any soft balls or scarves so
I had to use a toy monkey, a tennis ball and
a hard-boiled egg.

uh-oh

2. Mrs Duckworth came out of her house
and said, 'I hope you are not going to fling one
of those things at my window. It is only just
mended from when your father hit it with
a spanner.'

This made me lose concentration. The tennis ball whizzed one way, hitting Mrs Duckworth's window, and the hard-boiled egg whizzed the other way, landing on Topaz, who was sunbathing on the patio.

3. The hard-boiled egg turned out not to be so hard-boiled at all and splatted completely.

Topaz said I am ruining her life, i.e. she has to get a tan by tomorrow because she has realized that it is definitely the reason Garth Hunt kissed Shanice and not her. I told her sunbathing was dangerous for her skin, and she might die, but Topaz says if she doesn't kiss Garth, she will die anyway.

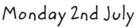

Monday 2nd July
Today a pigeon flew into my head in the playground and was so shocked it did a poo on my shoulder. Edward Bean said it was lucky and I should be pleased, but I do not see anything lucky about it at all because Lacey Prendergast saw me and started laughing like mad. Plus Elsie says now I might get a disease as pigeons are riddled with them.

Tuesday 3rd July

We learned about evacuation in school today, which is where all the children in big cities got sent away to live in the countryside. On Friday we have to dress like evacuees, i.e. in old-fashioned clothes and hats, and we have to bring a wartime lunch to school in a brown paper bag. I wish I really was being evacuated, only to the city instead of the countryside, as I have had enough of goats. And it would be safer, i.e. there would be no danger of Dad exploding the shed or taps pinging off or getting nits off Mum. Mr Atkins says I wouldn't really think that if it did happen because it was very upsetting for all the children not to see their mums and dads and even brothers and sisters, sometimes for years. But he hasn't met Topaz.

Plus I still haven't found my talent. I did try singing 'It's a Long Way to Tipperary' but not even Arnold Laine liked that. He actually went to hide in his pen so at least Mrs Duckworth is happy for once.

Wednesday 4th July

Trampolining is also not my talent.

When I got home from school, Dave the Rave was there helping Dad fiddle with a treadmill. I asked Dad what he was up to, but he said he couldn't tell me yet in case I sold his secret to a rival inventor. I said I don't know any inventors, and that includes him, which made Dave the Rave laugh, but Dad said I would be laughing on the other side of my face when he is on Best Business Brains on TV and to stop pestering him as I was interfering with his genius. He is not a genius and he is never going to be on Best Business Brains as you have to invent something that actually works.

I did stop pestering him because it turned out that, as well as the treadmill, Dave the Rave had brought round seventy-six tins of food (none of which have the labels on, which if you ask me is mad because what if you want e.g. baked beans and end up getting rice pudding) and a mini

MYSTERY TINS!

trampoline. So, I thought that maybe I could do trampolining tricks in the talent show, e.g. a somersault. And it started out quite well, i.e. I was jumping ever so high, only then I jumped so high I hit my head on a branch of the apple tree, and loads of apples fell onto the trampoline and started bouncing too, then I skidded on one and bounced right off onto the lawn.

Dave the Rave laughed on BOTH SIDES of his face and said I would be a brilliant circus act. I do not think it is funny at all, it is utterly trying.

Plus, to make matters worse, Arnold got excited about the apples and climbed onto the trampoline to eat them and now his hooves are stuck in the webbing and he is bouncing madly and bleating, and Mrs Duckworth is shouting that none of our family are normal.

For once I agree with her.

Thursday 5th July

Topaz is definitely not normal.

This morning she went to school looking her usual colour, i.e. not tanned, but when she got back at five she was bright orange. Dad said it was a miracle, and Mum said it was a mystery, but there is nothing mysterious at all – Suzy Gilhoolie has given her a fake tan, only she used double the amount to make sure, and so now Topaz looks like a walking satsuma.

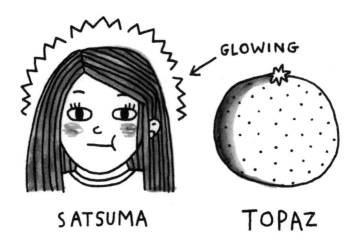

GLOWING

SATSUMA   TOPAZ

Friday 6th July

Mum has let Topaz stay off school until she fades a bit. I said that wasn't fair as she didn't have an actual disease, but Mum said it would be too embarrassing for her and people might laugh. I said she should try being her sister, i.e. me, as it is completely embarrassing, but Mum said she didn't have time to argue as she had to make a lobster costume for the nursery's end of term play. The lobster is going to be very disappointed if my evacuee costume is anything to go by. It is a skirt made out of a curtain and an old cushion cover for a hat.

5pm

I wish I had stayed off with Topaz. The only person who didn't laugh at my costume was Edward Bean. And it gets worse. Lacey said she was surprised I hadn't brought Arnold in to complete the look. Edward said, 'Who's Arnold?' and I said, 'No one', but Lacey said,

'I know,' and nudged Elsie. Elsie went red and looked at her feet as if they were the most interesting thing in the world, which they were not, because she had normal shoes on instead of wellies like me (because Mum said they were quite war-like and also because Arnold had chewed the buckle on my school shoes).

Maybe Topaz is right after all. Maybe it is the ultimate betrayal. It is certainly more than trying.

Saturday 7th July

My emergency replacement passport has still not arrived. Mum said she didn't know why I was so gloomy about it as I said I didn't even want to go to Florida because I would miss Elsie so much. I said circumstances had changed. Plus I am thinking of emigrating as living with Granny and Hank cannot be worse than living here. Topaz agrees. She said if she lived in Florida she wouldn't have had to use fake tan, and so it is all Mum and Dad's fault for living in Chipping Broadley, if you think about it. Dad says he has thought about it and he thinks she is crackers. And Mum says we wouldn't like it really because it is hot, even at night, and Hank walks the dog in his vest. But I said I have seen Dad go to the shops in his pyjamas before and Mum admitted this is true.

Sunday 8th July

It is now thirty-seven days since Elsie Eckersley has been to my house. Even Dad has noticed she is missing (because normally she is in the shed asking what he is inventing, and trying to persuade him to invent a machine that turns butter beans into chocolate biscuits). He said, 'What's up, kiddo?' I said I wasn't a kiddo, and that Elsie was just busy singing 'It's a Long Way To Tipperary' with Lacey Prendergast, because Lacey has NORMAL pets and NORMAL parents. He said it was a lucky escape for me because being normal is highly overrated. Then he went back to doing something with a hammer, wearing a pair of swimming trunks, a T-shirt that says 'I ♡ hippos' and a cowboy hat.

Just as I was about to beg him not to go to the shops dressed like that, the phone rang. Dad said, 'That'll be Elsie, mark my words.' So I did mark his words, which was a mistake because not only did I trip over his flip-flops on the way

DAD

COWBOY HAT!

BEWARE!

I ♥ HIPPOS

???→

SWIMMING TRUNKS!?

NOT NORMAL!

and fall into the lobster costume, completely crushing a claw; it wasn't Elsie, it was Edward Bean asking if I wanted to come over for tea. I said yes, because it was that or a tin of soup, and Mum doesn't even know what flavour it is, or even if it is soup, because it is one of the tins Dave the Rave brought round.

6pm

Being at Edward Bean's was actually sort of good. We made cookies, which were supposed to be just chocolate chip, but I told him about Everything Biscuits, so we also added marshmallows and a banana, which sounds disgusting but actually worked (unlike toothpaste and sultanas, which does not).

When I got back, Topaz was in a mood as the soup turned out to be peaches in syrup. I asked what pudding was. Dad said beef stew.

Monday 9th July

Topaz has gone back to school. She begged to stay off for another day, but Mum said she had faded enough, i.e. she is still orangey, but it is more the colour of our back fence rather than an actual satsuma. She says it will be all Mum's fault when she is in therapy for trauma at school.

Our school was completely traumatic today. It is partly because Brady O'Grady hit Luke Bruton on the head with a football (four times), so he got sent to see Mrs Hunderby. But mostly it was because of Lacey Prendergast. What

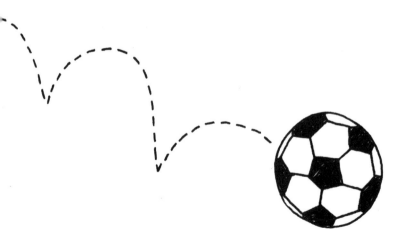

happened was that Edward Bean brought in some of the Everything Biscuits for his snack. Elsie asked what was in them and he told her and asked if she wanted to try one. She was going to say yes, but Lacey said, 'Ewwww, don't touch them, you'll catch the Dreaded Lurgy!' And even though Elsie knows Everything Biscuits don't have lurgy in them, she went 'Ewwww' too and ran away and so did everyone else. Edward didn't care. He just shrugged and said, 'Well, all the more for us, then.' But I wasn't hungry any more.

6pm

Now I wish I'd eaten the biscuit. Tea was potatoes (tinned) and custard (tinned), which do not go together, no matter what Dad says. At least  he didn't make us eat pudding though. That turned out to be cat food.

Tuesday 10th July

Topaz didn't moan about going to school, which Dad says is a miracle and Mum says is a mystery. It isn't mysterious. It is because she heard from Suzy Gilhoolie, who got it off Verity Jones, who got it off Charley, that Shanice and Garth have had an argument because he didn't take her to his nan's 60th birthday on Sunday. I said Shanice is crackers because who would want to go to the party anyway, especially if his nan has a moustache like Nanna Baxter. But Topaz said that is not the point and if you love someone you will go anywhere with them. I said, 'Even to an alligator-infested swamp?' and she said yes. I said, 'Even to a planet peopled entirely by monkeys?' She said yes. I said, 'Even to the most inhospitable place in the world, where you are guaranteed to get bitten by disease-carrying mosquitos and die a slow, horrible death?' She said yes and also to shut up.

I am never falling in love if it makes you go to swamps or 60th birthday parties.

Wednesday 11th July

An actual miracle has happened and it is nothing to do with Topaz. It is that Lacey Prendergast is off school! Brady O'Grady said it was probably rabies, and Luke Bruton said it was probably myxomatosis, and Edward Bean said she probably has the Dreaded Lurgy and that the biscuit might have cured it. But Mr Atkins says she doesn't have rabies or myxomatosis or Dreaded anything – she has a sore throat, and also that biscuits do not cure anything. Elsie said actually they do, e.g. if you have low blood sugar, but Mr Atkins said it was time to get out our workbooks and learn about land girls and if anyone mentioned any more diseases they would get sent to Mrs Hunderby.

Thursday 12th July

Lacey Prendergast is still off school. I said maybe the sore throat is actually the symptom of something else, and Elsie said it was definitely a possibility, e.g. an allergy to mites in the dust because even clean dust is full of invisible bugs. Then I said maybe she would like to come round to mine on Sunday as now she can't practise with Lacey because she might be contagious, and Elsie said OK then.

I will ask Mum if we can have fish fingers as I'm pretty sure Elsie will not want custard. Or cat food.

Friday 13th July

Mr Atkins reminded us that it is only a week now until the end of term, i.e. until: a) our project on being in the war has to be in and b) the Gang Show. Edward said we could work on the project on Sunday, but I said I couldn't because of Elsie coming round. He said that's a shame as he's going to interview his grandpa who was evacuated in the war. I said it was a shame as I would quite like to interview someone who was evacuated, but Elsie is more important.

Topaz is hoping Shanice will catch the sore throat, i.e. Lacey's big brother Lance Prendergast will give it to Julie Hunt, who will give it to her brother, Garth, who will give it to Shanice, then she will be off school and unkissable and Topaz can do the kissing instead. I said if Garth had given it to Shanice then he would be off school anyway, so they could still do kissing, but Topaz says Garth is so amazing not even a sore throat would stop him coming to school. He is mad.

I would stay off school next Friday even with a sore finger if I could.

Saturday 14th July
10am

This morning has been especially trying. It is Dad's fault, i.e. he woke everyone up at half past eight shouting from the garden that we had to come down immediately as he had something incredible to show us. Only when we got outside, all we could see was Arnold Laine, the treadmill and some cables, which Topaz said did not look very incredible, and I agreed. But Dad said, in fact, what we were looking at was his Patented Goat Generating Machine, i.e. he has rigged up the treadmill so that when Arnold walks on it, it creates energy, which gets converted in the motor to electricity and goes all the way from the cables to the kettle to boil a cup of tea, saving Mum from the horror of electricity bills.

Mum said she will believe it when she sees it,

so Dad said she can see it right now and made Arnold Laine climb on the treadmill. Only Arnold did not want to do any walking – he wanted to chew the rubber on the buttons, which didn't generate anything except a mess. We waited an hour, then Mum said she was gasping for a cuppa, and until Dad could persuade Arnold to move, it would be less horrifying to just turn on the kettle the normal way. So we all trooped inside.

12pm

Arnold Laine has still not walked anywhere.

3pm

Dad has now turned the treadmill on to encourage Arnold to walk. Arnold just started moving backwards like he was on an escalator and then fell off.

5pm

Dad is now on the treadmill and has been walking for half an hour. Mum said the kettle is not even close to boiling and it will take him all night to make a cup of tea, let alone power the fridge, the TV and the lights.

7pm

Dad is off the treadmill and back to the drawing board. It is because Mrs Duckworth said she was going to call the police if he didn't get off as the hoo-ha was distracting, plus Dad had taken off his 'I ♡ Hippos' T-shirt because he got so sweaty and was just in his shorts, which she said was unsightly and unhygienic.

I'm glad he stopped before Elsie comes round tomorrow. She might have found it unsightly too and gone straight to see Lacey, sore throat or not.

Sunday 15th July
10am
Elsie is late. She said she would come at half past nine and it is ten o'clock now and I have walked to the end of the road and I can't even see her coming down Dexter Drive.

11am
Elsie is still not here. Mum is going to phone the Eckersleys in case she has a sore throat.

11.10am
Elsie doesn't have a sore throat or a runny nose, or a cough, or any kind of Dreaded Lurgy. She has gone to Lacey's to catch up on rehearsals and stick sequins on their picture of wartime clothing. Mum said I should be working on my project anyway and, on the plus side, Elsie is going to get a bad mark if she thinks that anyone had sequins in the war, but I said that wasn't the point.

The point is, I wish she did have a lurgy. I wish

she had a lurgy that made her hair fall out and her nose turn purple and her feet go webbed like a duck's. Because now I am having the worst day ever.

11.30am

Maybe Mum was a bit right and I should be thinking about my project, i.e. go to Edward Bean's to see his grandpa after all.

It has to be better than here because now that his Patented Goat Generator has failed, Dad is trying to invent a machine than can automatically cut hair and give you a perm. I do not want either, especially not from something made from the vacuum cleaner and a pair of pinking shears.

5pm

Something definitely not trying has happened, and it is all thanks to Edward Bean. Or rather, Norman Bean, who is his grandpa. We went to his house on Beasley Street. It was full of war memorabilia, i.e. old stuff, including his gas mask, a ration book and a scarf that his mum knitted him when he left London to come here, which he has lent us for our project.

But that isn't the best bit. The best bit is that, as well as being an evacuee, Norman Bean was also once a magician called the Magical Marveloso. He showed us tricks with handkerchiefs AND silver rings AND a hat, which he pulled a biscuit out of (because he didn't have a rabbit). Then he let me have a go. I did a card trick and made a pound coin disappear and then found it in my ear, and pulled a handkerchief out of the hat (because Edward had eaten the biscuit).

It took about twenty goes to do them all, and Edward was laughing so much he spat biscuit

crumbs on me, but Norman says I definitely show potential as a performer. I said that is good as I do not show potential at anything else, i.e. at the Gang Show I am just going to have to stand there like a lemon and pretend that saying nothing is actually the most brilliant act ever. Which made Norman and Edward Bean laugh. Only Norman also had a better idea, which is to be the Mini Marveloso, i.e. I can borrow his tricks and do them at the Gang Show and I will win for sure because everyone loves magic.

I said there was no way
I would win because I
can't sing and I don't have
sequins. Plus it wasn't
about the winning, it was
about the joy, which made
Edward and Norman Bean
laugh again. But Edward
agreed with his grandpa.

He said magic tricks were better than singing.
Even better than multiplying 45 and 68 and if
I didn't do it then he would eat an Everything
Biscuit made of sardines and soap, which would
definitely not work, so I had to say yes.

I think I might have done it anyway because,
for the first time, trying out a talent wasn't trying
at all. It was sort of fun. So I have changed my
mind – today isn't the worst day ever, after all.
I mean, it's not the best day, because Topaz hasn't
been vaporized by aliens, but even so, it has been
pretty brilliant.

Monday 16th July

Elsie said sorry for not coming round yesterday, but I told her I couldn't care less, as she had done me a favour because now I had a talent for the Gang Show on Friday. She looked a bit sad and said, 'Really?' and I was about to say that actually I did care a bit, but Lacey Prendergast jabbed her with her elbow so she turned back round to concentrate on learning the 'Potato Pete' song which we are all singing as the Gang Show finale.

POTATO

It is a song about how nice potatoes are and how many different ways there are to eat them, which sounds crackers but I wish Mum would learn to do something apart from oven chips. Mum says in fact it is sexist to assume she should do the cooking, only the last time Dad did tea, the microwave blew up and we ended up eating cereal.

After the oven chips (and baked beans, which was the right tin for once, i.e. not mushroom soup or mandarins, so Dad shouted 'Bingo!'), I practised my magic tricks, i.e. I found two pounds in Topaz's ears and pulled one of Dad's socks out of the hat. Topaz says she should get the pounds as it was her ears, but Mum says she owes her for a T-shirt with a pair of lips on it, so she can have the sock if she wants, which she didn't.

Tuesday 17th July

I went to Edward Bean's after school to write up our project and also do more practising. He says it is a pity I don't have a real animal to pull out of the hat, so we tried to persuade a pigeon that was on his back wall to hop into it, but it just pecked it once then flew off to look at a crisp packet on the pavement. We're going to use his old toy rabbit instead, because even though it isn't real, at least it isn't one of Dad's socks.

Edward said I also need a volunteer to come up on stage and hold stuff and have the coins pulled out of their ears as that is what all real magicians do. I said what if no one volunteers to come up because they think I am weird, which they do, but he said then he will come up. It is a pact. Then he said I need to do a pact in return, i.e. I have to tell him what the P stands for in my name that I wrote on the front of our wartime project. I said, 'No way, José', but he said a deal is a deal. So in the end I said I would tell him, but only if I won a rosette, which there is no way I am going to, as Lacey has got real old-fashioned microphones and Brady O'Grady is bringing in his dog which can do backflips.

Wednesday 18th July

Mr Atkins says Brady can't bring in a dog, not even one that does backflips, as it is against school rules, and also Luke Bruton is allergic. Brady said he could have used his dog as a weapon in the war then, to kill all the allergic people, only Elsie said it is not like peanuts, i.e. you don't actually die from a dog allergy – you just sneeze a lot and itch. Brady said we should have used peanuts in the war then, so he got sent to Mrs Hunderby for being obsessed with weapons.

Thursday 19th July

Even without Brady's dog, there is no way I am going to win a rosette. In fact, according to Lacey, I am going to embarrass myself just by going up on stage and I might as well not bother. It's because she saw me and Edward practising with the hat behind the bike shed at break, only it was going wrong as every time I tried to pull the rabbit out of the hat, it got stuck, which was making Edward giggle. Only then I heard someone else sniggering, and when I turned round there was Lacey and Georgia-May and Elsie, all pointing and laughing. Well, Elsie wasn't pointing, but she wasn't telling Lacey to shut up either, which is almost as bad. Lacey said, 'You are hilarious, Ruby Baxter. I can't wait to see you do that on stage on Friday.' And then she and Georgia-May and Elsie walked off arm in arm, singing about packing up their troubles in their kitbags. I said I wished they would go to

Tipperary, and Edward said to ignore them and it will all be fine.

But I can't ignore them. Because when I got home and tried to pull a chocolate coin out of Arnold Laine's ear (because Dad has run out of real ones), it fell on the floor and he ate it, and then he bit the end off the wand as well. So now I am fed up, because without a wand I am not magic at all and Lacey is right, everyone will laugh.

Friday 20th July
8am

Lacey IS right. If I do the Gang Show I will die of embarrassment. There is nothing else for it, I am just going to have to stay at home. Me and Elsie have worked out how to do it without fake thermometer readings. You have to put some frozen peas on your face for a few minutes to make it cold and clammy, and then tip a glass of water down the loo and make horrid noises at the same time to pretend you are being sick. And the thing is, I do feel sick with nerves, so it is not even a complete lie.

Ruby P. Baxter
Beloved daughter and sister, died of embarrassment

8.30am

We have run out of peas, so I had to use a packet of fish fingers, which has made me smell slightly haddockish. But it still worked because Mum was busy being at the end of her tether so she just told me to go back to bed and Dad will have to be in charge.

Mum is going bonkers because my passport still hasn't arrived, which means we cannot fly to Gran's on Monday, which means Topaz says she is going to die because she is going to have to spend all summer in Chipping Broadley seeing Garth kissing Shanice because they have made up after the argument and were kissing in the spaghetti queue at lunch yesterday. I said to shut up because that was making me feel sick again (which wasn't a lie), but she said I was the one who had to shut up, because if I hadn't shown Arnold my passport he would never have eaten it in the first place, so it is all my fault. Then Mum told us both to shut up as she was on the phone to someone called Mrs Cement at the passport office, as well as trying to stick a pair of antennae on a sea snail costume for the end of year play because Alfie Garfunkel un-stuck them four times yesterday, and also hit Henry Dupree on the head with a plastic hammer.

Anyway, the point is, I'm not going to school, so I won't have to do the Gang Show, so I won't die of embarrassment. On the downside, Dad is in charge, but mostly he will be in the shed inventing things that don't work and I can just have toast for lunch because not even Dad can mess that up.

12.30 pm

Dad burnt the toast. Also four crumpets and two fish fingers, which I said shouldn't have gone in the toaster in the first place, but he said it is his new invention and will be a winner, I will see. Only now the toaster is broken and so he is back to the drawing board, and we are back to the weird tins, i.e. asparagus and rice pudding.

Dad said it's a shame I'm missing the Gang Show as it sounded terrific fun. I said it wouldn't be terrific fun, it would be terrifically trying and everyone would just laugh at me because I'm no good. He said that has never stopped him (not even when Mum laughed so much she couldn't breathe when he invented the Patented Combination Razor and Hairbrush and he ended up bald) because it is the trying that is the point. Plus when he does actually invent something that works, it will be all the more amazing. I said I couldn't even try anyway as I didn't have a wand any more, thanks to Arnold

Laine, but Dad said I could use anything for a wand, as the magic is in me, not in a stick. I said, 'Like what?' He said like his Patented Electric Fly Swat, which sparkles when you wave it through the air, only it is not actually meant to. Plus the flies do not get swatted as the holes in it are too big. But it does look cool.

So I tried it out on the toy rabbit in the hat, only the rabbit got stuck again four times, so by the end Dad was laughing instead of cheering. I said, 'See, I told you so.' But Dad said he wasn't laughing AT me, he was laughing WITH me because it was so clever. And in fact, it isn't the magic that is my talent, it is making people laugh. I said that isn't a talent, but he said the world was full of famous comedians and it could be the key to my fortune. But only if I start practising now, otherwise I will be wasting my talent, which is a crime (only not as bad as being a burglar). And then I had a terrible thought, that in fact I was wasting my talent right now, because the Gang Show starts in less than an hour and I am stuck here with a man who tries to toast fish fingers and a goat who eats passports.

And that is when I made a decision. Which is that I am going to do the Gang Show after all. Dad said he thought I had the Dreaded Lurgy, but I said I felt a lot better and it was probably the asparagus and he gave me a huge wink and said, 'Good luck, kiddo.' I said, 'Thanks, Daddio, I'll need it.'

Only now I am thinking maybe I need more than luck because I am about to stand up in front of everyone with a Patented Electric Fly Swat, some chocolate coins, a hat and a toy rabbit.

5pm

I did it! I did the Gang Show!

Lacey Prendergast said I should be disqualified for being late, but Brady O'Grady said she should be disqualified for being annoying, and Lacey said Brady should be disqualified for being a boy, and so Mr Atkins said no one was disqualified and to please hurry up and get on with it before the bell goes, and so I did.

When I did the coin trick, I deliberately made it go wrong, so that I couldn't find the coin behind Luke's ear, or Stephen Millican's ear, or even Edward's ear, as it was up Lacey's nose, which she said was mean, but everyone else said was genius and laughed loads. And then, when I was going to do the hat trick and I asked for an assistant, something even better happened. Because, instead of just Edward, everyone put up their hands (well, everyone except Lacey). Even Elsie. And when Lacey tried to pull her arm down, she stuck it up again even higher. When Edward saw Elsie put her hand up, he put his hand down and I felt bad. So in the end, I did something I never thought I would do. I picked him AND I picked Elsie. And they both held the hat while I yanked and yanked and yanked the rabbit so hard I fell over, and made everyone laugh so much Georgia-May Mannering was actually sick.

When Mr Atkins gave me my rosette, I said it was just luck that I had won, but Mr Atkins said it was more than that – it was talent and also the courage to be different. I said I'm actually not all that keen on being different, but he said I've done OK on it so far. And when I remembered everyone cheering, and Elsie and Edward standing next to me when I took a bow, I thought maybe, just maybe, he was right.

Epilogue: Saturday 28th July

The passport arrived this morning. But it turns out we're not going to Florida after all. Dad has actually sold one of his inventions, i.e. the Patented Banana Peeler, and he has to make four hundred and fifty of them by the end of August so he needs all of us to help. We had a party to celebrate, with actual food, i.e. hot dogs and corn on the cob and ice cream, as Mum said she is tired of Tin Bingo and has given the rest back to Dave the Rave.

Me, Edward and Elsie did make some Everything Biscuits though. And everyone loved the grape and ginger ones. But not even Arnold ate the ones with baked beans in.

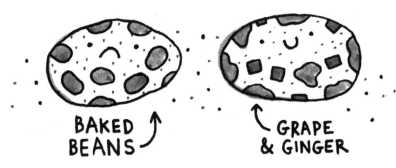

BAKED BEANS

GRAPE & GINGER

Topaz doesn't mind about not going to
Florida either. It's because Shanice broke up with
Garth at the end of term disco, because she says
he dances like a flamingo. I said that was good
because now Topaz could go out with him, but
she said, 'Ugh, as if!' Because now they are both
in love with Julian Brewster, who has seen Pink
Lemonade in concert four times, and can do
one-minute wheelies on his bicycle.

They are both crackers. Boys are worse than
the Dreaded Lurgy.

Except Edward Bean, of course.

He says he can't believe I never let him come
to my house before because it's the best house
ever, especially Arnold Laine and the Patented
Goat Generator. We all got on it – me, Edward
and Elsie – to see if we could make enough
electricity for a cup of tea, and we could, which
Dad said proves that friends are the important
ingredient to any invention.

And while we were all on the treadmill,

Edward reminded me about our pact, i.e. that I had to tell him what the P stood for in my name. And I was about to tell him, because a deal is a deal, when I had a better idea. I said, if he guessed it, then he could be in mine and Elsie's gang forever. So far he has tried Penelope, Patricia and Pixie. He is never going to get it.

But I'm pretty sure we'll let him in anyway.

And do you know what? Today really has been the Best Day Ever. Elsie said I shouldn't speak too soon, because she heard off Deirdre Riley, who heard it off Luke Bruton, who heard it off Mrs Buttons, who is the school secretary, that Lulu Webster-Price is coming back to our school next term, which would be exceedingly trying. Only I think I can handle it, which I was just about to tell her, when Mrs Duckworth stuck her head over the fence because Arnold Laine had got into her geraniums again. She took one look at us on the Patented Goat Generator and said, 'Ruby P. Baxter, you are just not NORMAL.'

And I said, 'I know! Brilliant, isn't it?!'

And it wasn't even a lie.

About the author

I have written nearly forty
books for children, including the bestselling
Rachel Riley series and the award-winning
Penny Dreadful series. I was a journalist as
well as a special adviser to the Prime Minister.
I live in Bath with my daughter, Millie, who
sometimes reminds me of Ruby P. Baxter.

As a child, I thought my family were utterly
normal and tedious, whereas my best friend
Aidan lived in a weird and wonderful house
with its own castle and lots of animals.
Ruby P. Baxter is the kind of girl I would've
loved to have been friends with. And before
you ask, I absolutely cannot tell you what the
P stands for!